FOR DAVID

First published 2016 by Walker Books Ltd

87 Vauxhall Walk, London SE11 5HJ 10 9 8 7 6 5 4 3 2 1

© 2016 Jenni Desmond The right of Jenni Desmond to be identified as author/illustrator

of this work has been asserted by her in accordance with the Copyright, Designs and Patents Act 1988

a catalogue record for this book is available from the British Library. ISBN 978-1-4063-6247-3 www.walker.co.uk

WALKER BOOKS
AND SUBSIDIARIES
LONDON · BOSTON · SYDNEY · AUCKLAND

ALBERT'S TREE

JENNI DESMOND

Spring arrived and Albert
woke from his long sleep.
"Hooray!" he shouted. As the snow was
quietly turning to water and trickling down from
the mountains, Albert raced to his favourite place.

His tree.

"Hello, Tree!" shouted Albert.
"I've missed you."
His tree was perfect.
Not too hard, or too soft,
or too slippery, or too prickly.

It was his own special place,
quiet and peaceful…

But what was that noise?

Albert's tree was crying.
"Waa!" wailed the tree.
"What's going on?" said Albert.
"You don't normally make a noise.

SNIFF
SNIFF

BOUNCE

You smell the same.

You feel the same.

And you taste
just the same,
even upside down."

"What are you doing,
Albert?" said Rabbit.

BOING BOING BOING BOING BOING

"Rabbit!" said Albert. "My tree is
crying! How can I cheer it up?"
"Waa, waa, waa!" wailed the tree.

"When I'm sad I dig lots of holes
to play in," said Rabbit helpfully.
"Maybe that will stop your tree crying."

So Albert and Rabbit dug lots of holes.

I didn't know
trees cried

"We've dug you some
holes to play in, Tree,"
said Albert.
But the tree just kept crying.
"Waa, waa, waaaa!" it wailed.

WAA

Along came Caribou.
"What are you doing,
Albert?" he said.

What's that
noise?

"My tree is crying. I'm trying to cheer it up," said Albert. "Well when I'm sad I eat grass," said Caribou.

So Albert and Caribou gathered lots of grass.

WAA

WAAA

WAAAA

yum yum

"We've brought you some grass, Tree," said Albert. "Please cheer up." But the tree just kept wailing.

"Why is your tree crying, Albert?" said Squirrel. "I don't know," sighed Albert.

The tree cried harder than ever.
"Pleeeease don't cry!" shouted Albert.
"WAA, WAA, WAAAAA!" wailed the tree.

"This noise is too much," said the others.

"PLEASE STOP IT, TREE," roared Albert. "STOP CRYING!"

But the louder he roared, the more the tree wailed.

"WAA! WAA! WAAAAAAAAAAA!"

Then Albert had one last idea.

He took a deep breath and
climbed quietly up to his
favourite branch. He wrapped
his thick furry paws around
the trunk and gave the tree
a huge, kind, bear hug.
He whispered in his tiniest voice,
"Why are you crying, Tree?"

To Albert's surprise, his tree whispered back, "Because I'm scared of the big hairy monster."

"What big hairy monster?" whispered Albert.

"Outside, over there," sobbed his tree.

"Don't worry. I'll get rid of it," said Albert bravely.

Albert nervously looked high
and low, outside and over there.
There was no monster.

"There's only me
here," said Albert.
"Oh, phew!" sniffed the tree.
"I can come out then."

A A R H !

screamed a tiny
feathered thing.
"You're the monster!"

AAARH!

screamed Albert.
"You're the tree!"

"I'm not a monster," said Albert.
"I'm Albert!"
"And I'm not a tree," said Owl. "I'm Owl."
Albert and Owl laughed and laughed
at their mistake.

ha

ha

ha

They both felt MUCH better.

Albert was glad his
tree was back to normal.
He and Owl played in it
all afternoon.

woah!

woah!

And as he watched Owl swooping from his favourite
branch, Albert knew that Owl loved the tree as much
as he did. Which, he secretly decided …

made his tree twice as perfect
as it was before.